117605 EN
The Three Snow Bears

Brett, Jan
B.L.: 3.1
Points: 0.5   LG

P9-CJH-246

JAN BRETT

THE THREE SNOW BEARS

G. P. PUTNAM'S SONS

For Katie

With thanks to the Brookfield Zoo

G. P. PUTNAM'S SONS A division of Penguin Young Readers Group. Published by The Penguin Group. Penguin Group (USA) Inc., 375 Hudson Street, New York, NY 10014, U.S.A. Penguin Group (Canada), 90 Eglinton Avenue East, Suite 700, Toronto, Ontario, Canada M4P 2Y3 (a division of Pearson Penguin Canada Inc.). Penguin Books Ltd, 80 Strand, London WC2R 0RL, England. Penguin Ireland, 25 St. Stephen's Green, Dublin 2, Ireland (a division of Penguin Books Ltd.). Penguin Group (Australia), 250 Camberwell Road, Camberwell, Victoria 3124, Australia (a division of Pearson Australia Group Pty Ltd). Penguin Books India Pvt Ltd, 11 Community Centre, Panchsheel Park, New Delhi - 110 017, India. Penguin Group (NZ), 67 Apollo Drive, Mairangi Bay, Auckland 1311, New Zealand (a division of Pearson New Zealand Ltd.) Penguin Books (South Africa) (Pty) Ltd, 24 Sturdee Avenue, Rosebank, Johannesburg 2196, South Africa. Penguin Books Ltd, Registered Offices: 80 Strand, London WC2R 0RL, England.

Manufactured in China by South China Printing Co. Ltd. Design by Marikka Tamura. Text set in Della Robbia. The art was done in watercolors and gouache. Airbrush backgrounds by Joseph Hearne.
Library of Congress Cataloging-in-Publication Data available upon request.
ISBN 978-0-399-24792-7
1 2 3 4 5 6 7 8 9 10
FIRST IMPRESSION

"Come back!" Aloo-ki shouted as her huskies floated out to sea. *Oh, no!* She knew that although an ice floe is a good place to fish, it is a bad place to lose a dog team.

Not far away a snow bear family had just started to eat their breakfast. But it was way too hot for Baby Bear.

"Ow-ee!" yowled
Baby Bear. "My breakfast
burned my mouth."
"We'll go for a stroll
and let the soup cool,"
Mama Bear said.

Aloo-ki was running along looking for her dogs when she came upon the biggest igloo she had ever seen.

Who lives here? she wondered.

Aloo-ki ducked inside. Right away,
she smelled something delicious.

Across the room, she saw a big bowl,
a middle-sized bowl, and a small bowl.
Surely the good smell was coming from
the three bowls.

Aloo-ki took a sip from the biggest bowl.
"Owwwwww!" she cried out. "Too hot!"
She took a sip from the middle-sized bowl.
"Ewwwwww! Too cold!"
She tipped up the littlest bowl and drank every drop.
"Mmmmmm!" she said. "Not too hot and not too cold."

In the next room Aloo-ki spotted three pairs of beautiful boots standing in a row.

She put on the biggest boot. "Too big!" she said.

She put on the middle-sized boot. "Too fancy!" she said.

She put on the littlest pair. "Just right!" she said, wiggling her toes in the soft fur lining.

Aloo-ki walked into the last room and found a long sleeping bench piled high with fur covers. Heat from an oil lamp warmed her cheeks and made her sleepy. *Time for a nap,* she thought.

She crawled under the highest mound of covers. "Too lumpy," she grumbled. She tried the middle bed with the furry fringe cover, but sank down so far that she could hardly breathe. "Too soft," she said.

She rolled over into the smallest sleeping place. The furry blanket was cozy and warm and the pillow was just her size.

"Just right," Aloo-ki murmured and was asleep before she could take her boots off.

If Aloo-ki hadn't fallen fast asleep, she might have heard her dogs barking happily.

Papa Bear, Mama Bear, and Baby Bear
had spotted them adrift in the strong current
and gone out to save them. The snow bear
family was pushing Aloo-ki's dog team back
toward their igloo and safety.

Papa Bear crawled into the igloo and saw
his big bowl sitting in a pool of spilled soup.
"Someone has been tasting my soup!" he roared.

Mama Bear rushed in and saw that her soup
had been sloshed around too. "Someone has been
sipping my soup," she growled.

"Someone found my soup!" sputtered Baby Bear
in her high, squeaky voice. "And they ate it all up!"

Papa Bear ran into the next room and saw his boots in the middle of the floor. "Someone has been trying on my boots," he boomed in his big bear voice.

Mama Bear put on her fancy boots. "Someone has had these boots on," she huffed, "and the fur is all bunched up."

Baby Bear saw that her boots had disappeared. "Someone has taken my boots and left behind these not as good ones!" she wailed.

The bears ran into
their bedroom.

"Someone has been sleeping in my bed!" Papa Bear bellowed.

"Someone has been sleeping in my bed too!" Mama Bear cried.

Baby Bear peeked at her little bed and squeaked, "Someone has been sleeping in my bed, and here she is!"

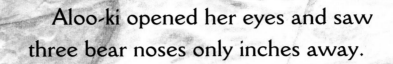

Aloo-ki opened her eyes and saw
three bear noses only inches away.

She hopped out of bed and
dove between Papa Bear's
huge furry LEGS!

Quicker than a seal, Aloo-ki
ran from room to room until she
burst outside.

Her huskies bounced around, barking
and smiling their doggy grins.

Aloo-ki and her dogs flew over the frozen ice,
dodging ridges and cracks. She looked back
to wave a thank-you to the snow bears.

She couldn't see them, but she heard a big gruff
voice, a middle-sized voice, and a high, squeaky
voice calling to her . . .